Jerry Perlet's Dragon Stories:

Sara's Adventures with the Dragon

JERROLD PERLET

To the students of

Monocacy Elementary School

And

Sherwood Elementary School

Copyright 2013

Second Edition 2015

Author's Notes

Jerry Perlet's Dragon Stories, Sarah's Adventures with the Dragon is a compilation of many years of storytelling about the dragon who lives on the mountain and befriends the children. The first dragon story was told to a group of students at Monocacy Elementary School as they waited for a late bus. The setting comes from Sugarloaf Mountain and the many farmhouses in the area. The adventures with the dragon were created as a part of the quarterly school assemblies. As I moved to Sherwood Elementary School, I shared the stories there as well. The children and their parents often asked where they could buy the book that I was telling the stories from. I explained that they came out of my head as I told them and there was no book.   Many families have asked to have the tales written out.

Over the years, the students have asked many questions and contributed many ideas to the stories. There are so many now that I have divided them into two volumes. The first is **Sara's Adventures with the Dragon** followed by **George and Zoe's Adventures with the Dragon**. These adventures led to volumes three, four, and five.

I have retired from the Montgomery County Public schools in Maryland after 38 years in teaching and as an elementary principal. I have also published two novels in the Grandpa Ek series, **Adventures with Grandpa Ek: Washingon DC** and **Adventures with Grandpa Ek: Annapolis**. These are also available at Amazon.com. Many other stories are in their beginning stages to be released in the future.

I hope you will enjoy the adventures!

Jerry Perlet   GrandpaEk@yahoo.com

Special Thanks to:

Marie Perlet, my wife and my editor

Katie and Matthew Perlet for designing the covers

Table of Contents

There's No Such Thing As A Dragon!

It was a dark and stormy summer night with a driving rain. Thunder and lightning crashed about the house silhouetting the mountain with each flash. The three children were getting ready for bed and they went to the window to watch the storm. They were amazed by the bright flashes of lightning.

As the lightning flashed across the mountain, Sara saw a strange blue light glowing along the mountain trail. "Look! What do you think that is?"

All three decided they needed to find out what that glowing blue light was, so they put on their raincoats, grabbed their flashlights, and went out on the muddy trail. As they climbed the mountain, the rain came down and the thunder roared above their heads. The trail was so muddy they often slipped as they climbed.

Sara, Matt, and Tom reached a large boulder in the path and the blue glowing light became brighter. It seemed to have a slow, pulsating rhythm to it. The boys led the way up to the boulder and then stopped. "Should we go ahead?" they asked Sara.

"Of course. What do you think we're gonna find, a dragon or something?"

"Why don't you go first?" they suggested.

"All right you 'fraidy cats. I'll go first!"

And so Sara led the way and the three rounded the boulder. Lying there in the path was a huge dragon almost 15 feet long! He was glowing a blue color and he looked very sick. The dragon was moaning and his tongue was hanging out of his mouth. The children rushed through the mud to the dragon's side. "Oh, Mr. Dragon, what is the matter with you?"

The rain came down and the thunder and lightning continued. The dragon moaned again. "Dear children, I have eaten some red berries that have made me very sick. I am losing my magical powers. My stomach hurts so badly."

The children were amazed at the size of the dragon and they wanted to help him. Sara stood up and said, "I know what to do. I'll be right back."

She raced down the muddy trail and back into the house. She ran to the bathroom medicine cabinet and got the bottle of that pink stuff for upset stomachs and ran back to the mountain. Rain was coming down even harder now. Lightning was crashing and the trail was a muddy mess, but she ran ahead determined to help the dragon.

Tom and Matt were sitting next to the moaning dragon telling him everything would be OK as soon as their sister returned. She always knew what to do. Sara came up to the dragon and gave him the bottle. "Since you're so big, you should drink the whole bottle. You'll feel better in no time!"

The dragon eyed the pink liquid and then with one big gulp he emptied the bottle. As the children watched over him, he began to return to his natural color, a beautiful green hue. The children were amazed as he changed. Gradually his arms and legs began to move and soon he sat up and spread his wings. "I feel so much better. Thank you, children. Let me stop this crazy storm." The dragon pointed at the sky with his large claw. The children couldn't believe what they saw happen. The rain stopped, the clouds blew away, and the stars came out. "There, that's much better!"

The dragon turned to the children. "May I ask who you are and where you are from?"

"Mr. Dragon, my name is Sara and these are my two younger brothers, Tom and Matt. We live in the old farmhouse down there below the mountain. We come here all the time. This is one of our most favorite places. But we have never seen you here before. Who are you and where did you come from?"

"I am the dragon and I don't really have a name or a home. I wander the earth looking for friends and a place to call home."

"Well, you've come to the right place, Mr. Dragon! This mountain is a terrific place to live and we'll be your friends. What kind of a house do you live in?"

"Sara, dragons don't live in houses!" Tom pointed out. "They live in caves and we have never found any caves here on this mountain."

The dragon thought Sara's invitation was a marvelous idea. "Children, this is terrific! I have found some great friends and a wonderful place to live. I will find a cave and then you can visit me."

"But how will we find your cave?" asked Matt. "And how will we know where to find you?"

"Do you see that big oak tree in your backyard?" The dragon pointed to their backyard and the large oak tree began to glow! The children stared with large eyes. "Whenever you want to come see me, knock three times on the tree and a magic door will open. Climb down the spiral stairs and follow the yellow path to my cave. I will be there waiting for you. Now you need to get home to bed and get some rest. Tomorrow will be another exciting day and I will see you soon. And thank you so much for coming to my rescue."

The children said goodbye to the dragon and climbed down the muddy trail to their house. They hung their wet clothes in the bathroom and climbed into their beds. Matt asked, "Did we really see a dragon tonight, or have I been dreaming?"

"Well, if we imagined this, then we were all dreaming," Sara said as she drifted off to sleep. "There was the rain, the thunder and lightning, and that muddy path! I think we found a sick dragon and made him well. We'll try the oak tree in the morning and we'll see if we have found a new friend."

The children fell asleep dreaming of the amazing adventures they would have with their dragon. And that is how they met the dragon who lives on their mountain. They couldn't wait for Saturday to see if the tree really had a magic door.

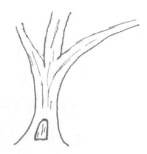

The First Visit to the Dragon's Cave

It was a beautiful Saturday morning in June, the first Saturday after the big storm. The sky was a brilliant blue and the sun was shining brightly. "It's a beautiful day! Let's go find the dragon and his cave!"

The children jumped out of bed, got dressed quickly, and dashed down to breakfast. Mom had made their favorites. They gobbled down a huge pile of pancakes with lots of gooey syrup and gulped down big glasses of orange juice. The children thanked their mom for a great breakfast and off they went to the big old tree in the backyard. As they approached the tree, they tried to remember what the dragon had told them when they met him on the mountain in the storm.

"He said to knock three times on the tree. Let's see if it works."

Sara knocked on the tree three times and a magic door opened in the side of the tree. As the children ran inside, the door closed behind them. They went down a spiral staircase and reached a glowing yellow pathway. "This is it. He said that we just follow the yellow path."

Matt and Tom led the way up the path and the children reached the dragon's cave in a short time. A large wooden door was wide open and the children peeked inside. The dragon was sitting in his big rocking chair reading the morning newspaper. "Well, well, good morning children and welcome to my cave."

"This is cool, Mr. Dragon. How did you find this cave?"

"You know that dragons have magical powers and I created this cave with my magic. These yellow crystals light the cave and I can wave my hand to make it brighter or darker." The dragon showed the children with his large claw.

Then the dragon led the children on a tour of the cave. "Here I have a kitchen to cook my dragon stews in this big black pot. There are enough chairs for us all to sit and enjoy our stew. Over there I have a library full of good books and this is my bedroom."

As the children wandered through the cave they were amazed at the size of the furniture. Of course the dragon was more than 15 feet tall, so they realized he needed big furniture. They could tell they would visit this cave often and they would have great adventures with the dragon.

"What shall we do today?" the dragon asked.

The children explained to the dragon that during the summer they loved to go swimming in the pond at the nearby farm. The dragon agreed that it was getting hot and a good swim would be a nice way to cool off. Dragons don't usually have air conditioning in their caves!

So the children climbed on the dragon's back and they flew up out of the cave high into the sky. They spotted the farmer's pond and pointed to it. The dragon swooped down to the pond and landed on the shore. "This is a lovely pond, children. Is the water cold?"

The children giggled and said, "No, it's not TOO cold!" Even though they did not have their swimsuits, they jumped into the water in their summer clothes. They floated about on their backs, laughing and splashing water at each other. "Come on, Mr. Dragon! Aren't you going to come in too?"

The dragon eyed the water suspiciously and then put one claw into the water. He quickly pulled back and shouted, "The water is too cold! How can you splash about in such cold water?"

The children giggled again and said, "Come on in. You get used to the cold water and then you just don't feel it!"

So the Dragon did a giant belly flop into the pond. Well, of course, a big 15 foot dragon will make a BIG splash and water went everywhere! In fact half the pond flew up into the air and then crashed back into the pond showering all of them with water. Suddenly a group of catfish came to the surface and began yelling at the children and the dragon. "What are you doing in our pond making such a noise and such a mess?!" The children apologized and said they would be quieter. The catfish dove below before the dragon saw them and could have them for his lunch! The dragon just floated about sighing and cooling off. The dragon and the children laughed and played for a long while.

Finally everyone was tired and it was time to go. "How will we get dried off?" the children asked. The dragon said he would breathe some warm air on them and that would dry them off. So the dragon took a deep breath and carefully let out some warm air. It was like a hair dryer and the children dried very quickly!

The children clambered onto the dragon's back and away they flew to the cave. The dragon served the children some of his yummy snail cookies which really didn't taste all that bad. He also had some bug juice that tasted a lot like Koolaid. Everyone talked about their adventure at the pond and the silly catfish who kept complaining about their splashing about. The dragon said that he would have caught them and brought them home for his dinner if he had known they were there. The children were glad that the dragon did not see the fish!

It was time to go, so the children waved goodbye to the dragon and thanked him for a great day. They ran down the yellow pathway to the staircase and climbed up to the secret door. Sara opened the door and they ran to the house. They dashed into the kitchen just in time for dinner. Mother asked, "Where have you been all day?"

The children all began talking at once telling about the pond and the catfish and swimming and the dragon doing a giant belly flop and splashing all the water in the air. And Mother looked at the children and said, "Children, there's no such thing as a dragon!"

The Wrong Pathway

It was another one of those great Saturdays when the world just seemed right for an adventure. The children jumped out of bed, got dressed in their adventure clothes, and dashed down to breakfast. They enjoyed a large pile of pancakes with lots of gooey syrup and a big glass of orange juice. They thanked their mom and ran to the magic tree. They knocked three times on the trunk and the magic doorway opened. They raced down the spiral staircase and started up the yellow path to the dragon's cave.

But today there was something different. As they approached a bend in the yellow pathway, they discovered a new pathway that they had never seen before. This path glowed blue instead of the regular yellow.

"Hey, let's go check this out!" Tom shouted.

Matt said, "No, the dragon told us to stay on the yellow path and not to go anywhere else." Sara nodded her head in agreement.

"Ah, come on you chickens. What could possibly be down there and what could possibly happen?"

"I don't know what could be down there, but if the dragon said to stay on the yellow pathway, who knows what could be down there? We didn't think there was a dragon and then we discovered him! What else could there be?"

"Well, there's only one way to find out. Let's go!" And off Tom went down the blue path. Matt and Sara were very worried about this, so they reluctantly followed him down the path. As they moved along there was some pretty music playing and the air smelled of chocolate. This seemed to be getting better and better and Matt and Sara began to relax as Tom raced ahead. They came to a bridge and there was a big sign that said **"BEWARE! DO NOT CROSS THIS BRIDGE!"**

Sara said, "Hmmmm, I think we better head back now." Matt agreed.

But Tom said, "I came this far, I'm going to see what is across this bridge."

Sara and Matt objected, but Tom dashed across the bridge jumping up and down on the path and laughing. "It's great over here! I feel soooo good! Come on and have some fun!" His eyes were really large and he was acting really goofy. Sara and Matt were quite alarmed. They yelled at him to come back. He just laughed more and danced off the path. All of a sudden he stopped.

"Hey! I can't move! My feet are stuck in this thick brown mud! I can't move!" Tom became very upset and every time he tried to move, his feet sank deeper into the mud.

Sara yelled at him, "Stand still! Don't keep moving! Every time you wiggle you sink deeper! We need to figure out what to do!" Matt and Sara looked about for anything that might help. They couldn't find anything.

Matt said, "We have to get the dragon! You stay here and I'll go get him." He ran back up the pathway as Sara talked quietly to Tom, stuck in the mud.

"You need to stand still and stop moving. Matt went to get the dragon and he will help us out."

"No, not the dragon! He will be so disappointed with me!"

"Oh well, we don't have any other ideas how to help you out."

"Can't you find anything to pull me out of here?"

"There is nothing on this pathway. I don't know what is to the left or the right, but I don't want get off the path and get stuck myself. Just stand still until the dragon gets here."

It was a long ten minutes waiting for Matt to return with the dragon. They came down the path and the dragon was just shaking his head. "Didn't I tell you not to leave the yellow pathway? This is the land of the Mucklucks. They like to have children for dinner and I don't mean as guests! They set traps with yummy odors and lovely music and then when the children are least expecting it, they step into the mud. It is very hard to escape from the mud, so listen to me carefully before the Mucklucks come for you."

The dragon told Sara and Matt to back up. He climbed onto the bridge. He reached out his claw and told Tom to grab on. Then he breathed fire down onto the mud and pulled with all of his might and slowly Tom rose up out of the mud. He finally popped out of the mud with a big whoosh and the dragon lifted him over the bridge to the pathway with his brother and sister.

As the dragon backed over the bridge, a big hairy Muckluck came clomping down the path. "What are you doing on my path!?" he shouted. "Dragons are not allowed down here and you know it!"

"We were just leaving!" the dragon bellowed back at the Muckluck. "Run up the path, children, and move to the cave." The children ran as fast as they could to the yellow path. They heard the dragon and the Muckluck yelling at each other and as they looked back they could see the Muckluck throwing chunks of mud at the dragon. The dragon shot flames at each chunk to disintegrate them. The dragon slowly backed up the blue path towards the children. They did not wait to be told again and they ran for the cave.

When the dragon arrived in the cave, he was pretty tired and he had two spots on his back where the mud had landed. The mud had caused sores on his back. He was not a happy dragon. "What were you thinking? You could have been dinner for that Muckluck. Thank goodness your brother could run so fast!"

"I am so, so sorry Mr. Dragon! It was a really stupid thing to do! I have really learned a lesson from this. I am not going down paths that I don't know something about and I am going to read signs and do what they tell me!"

Sara asked the dragon how she could help with the sores on his back. He asked her to get a large red jar off the shelf and rub some of the cream on the sores. As she did this, the sores disappeared and the dragon felt better. Matt was busy in the dragon's kitchen making some hot chocolate for everyone. He also found some large chocolate chip cookies and brought them out with the hot chocolate. Everyone settled down on the couch to eat their cookies and hot chocolate.

The muddy brother was very ashamed and sat on the end of the couch with his head down. He couldn't eat or drink. The dragon spoke kindly to him. "Tom, you gave us all a big scare and we care about you, and so we got angry that you would do something so silly, so dangerous. I am sorry if

I yelled at you. Do you understand why I told you to stay on the yellow path?"

Tom nodded his head and said, "I am really sorry everybody. I was not thinking." Everyone gave him a hug and told him it was OK and that he should eat his cookie and drink his chocolate. He felt better and ate and drank.

"When you children want an adventure, you must take me along. I know the tricks and the dangerous places. I can protect you and guide you. You can explore the unknown, but you must use caution and think carefully watching for the signs. I can teach you these things, but we must go together."

The children were glad to have a friendly dragon who could teach them so much about the world and how to walk the dangerous paths safely. After a while they decided to head home. They all thanked the dragon and he gave the muddy brother a hug and sent them on their way. They walked back up the yellow path and did not even see the blue path anymore. They reached the stairway and climbed it carefully to the top. They dashed out of the tree and raced for home.

As they came running into the kitchen, their Mother told them to stop and get all those muddy clothes off in the laundry room. Then they ran into the kitchen to tell their Mother about their adventure. Everything sounded pretty real until they said that a dragon had saved them. Then Mother said, "There's no such thing as a dragon."

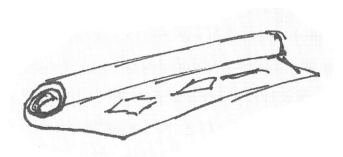

Summertime Projects

It was a hot and humid Saturday morning in early August. The children jumped out of bed, got dressed quickly, and dashed down to breakfast. Mom had made their favorites. They gobbled down a huge pile of pancakes with lots of gooey syrup and gulped down big glasses of orange juice. Then Mom reminded them that they had to begin to prepare for the first days of school by completing some reading and math each day.

"Ah Mom, do we have to? Summer is our play time!"

"Yes, but you need to keep in practice so that the first days of school go smoothly. You don't have to work on the weekends, but next week you will need to begin studying."

After a bit more mumbling about schoolwork, the children thanked their mom for a great breakfast and off they went to the big old tree in the backyard. They knocked on the tree three times, the magic door opened, and they were off down the spiral staircase and up the yellow pathway to the dragon's cave. They burst into the cave and found the dragon busy reading his morning newspaper.

"Good morning and how are we all doing today?"

"Well, we were doing just fine until Mom said we had to start studying for school. We don't want to have to sit down and do all these worksheets. They are so boring!"

"We have had a great summer! We got to sleep late and do whatever we wanted and we've had lots of fun."

"Yeah, and we got to play outside all day, climb trees, and splash in the stream."

"And we didn't have any homework!"

"Sounds like you have had lots of fun," the dragon replied. "Seems like you don't want to do any schoolwork?"

"Yeah! It's still vacation!"

"Yes, well, I can see why you might not want to do too much schoolwork, but I know that you have to practice some reading and math every day so that you don't forget it. If you don't do any work over the summer, you will go back to school weak in your head and your classmates will be way ahead of you."

Matt looked at the dragon. "Yeah, we know we need to study, but I guess we were hoping for a few more weeks of fun."

The dragon looked over his spectacles at the three sullen children. "I'm glad that you know it is important to learn how to read and to be able to do math. But you don't always have to do worksheets to practice your skills. There are fun ways to practice, too."

Sara said, "The dragon just said that practicing our skills could be fun. I want to hear what he is thinking about."

The children settled down around the dragon to hear his plan.

"The important thing about learning to read and do math is what you are going to use it for. Why do you go to school and learn all of this information?"

Tom spoke up, "Because as we grow up we need to be able to read and do math for the many jobs and activities that we need to do as adults. We can't run a household or do a job without some skills."

Matt added, "I want to be a doctor when I grow up and I know I will need to be able to read about diseases and medicines and do all kinds of math to figure out how to help my patients."

"And I want to be an architect and design houses. I guess I need to know a lot about math so that the building doesn't fall down," Sara explained.

"These are all important reasons to learn, but it is also your human nature to want to explore and learn about your world. Learning is something your brain wants to do. You are naturally curious. A good way to keep your brain sharp is to work on some project that is interesting to you and uses your skills. So let's make a list of projects that you would like to work on before school starts and then figure out what school skills you can practice as you do the projects."

They made a list of several possibilities, but the group all seemed to agree that re-building the old tree fort near their house was number one on the list. "We need to get that fort into shape so we can use it."

The dragon was pleased that they wanted to get the old tree house in order since he knew it would be important in the future. He agreed and showed the children several books about tree houses including Swiss Family Robinson and Robinson Caruso. He asked Sara to plan out the project with Matt and Tom. They settled down on the floor of the cave with the books and several pieces of big paper and markers and designed the tree house. After about an hour, they presented their plans to the dragon.

"We want to have one big room where we can spread out and play board games when it rains. But then have a cupboard where we can put the games so we can use the space to play pirates and other action games. And then when it snows we want to be able to bring up lots of snow to make snowballs and have big fights, so we think we need some kind of an elevator to move the snowballs and other things up into the fort."

"We thought the Swiss Family Robinsons had a lot of cool ideas that we can do once we have the basic fort built."

"And we want a nice big window that looks out on the mountain so that we can always look up here to check on you!"

The dragon reviewed the drawings. They were pretty detailed with many labels and explanations. "So you just used your reading and writing skills to produce this plan. When you show it to your parents what else will you need?"

Matt offered up they would need to know what materials were necessary to build the fort. And Tom added that they would have to do some measuring and then order enough of the materials. Sara pointed out that parts of the old fort were still in the tree and they would have to ask their parents to check this out and decide if they could use any of it. And they might need some help with some of the tools and the heavy lifting.

"So you have a lot of planning and measuring to do, then designing a detailed plan to present and hopefully convince your parents to do the project. Anything else?"

"How about a budget"?" Tom pointed out. "How much will it cost and who will pay for it?"

The children worked for the remainder of the afternoon. At one point they asked the dragon to fly them to the old fort and keep them safe while they checked out some things. They measured how big the fort should be and noted that all the old fort timbers seemed to be pretty rotten. After their visit they were able to make a list of materials. Matt said he could get the prices on the Internet when they got home.

After a long day of hard work, the children waved goodbye to the dragon and headed home with all of their plans. They burst into the kitchen just in time for dinner. Their Dad was home early and they began to present their plan before dinner even reached the table. They explained every detail and their parents were very impressed. Mom pointed out that they were using many of their math and reading skills and this would be a great way to practice to get ready for school. Dad agreed to pay for the materials and to be available if they needed help with the heavy lifting.

Mom commented she remembered playing in the fort with her brother Richard when they were young. It was a good idea. Then their parents asked, "Where did you come up with this idea?"

The children all said together, "The dragon thought of this and helped us get started!"

Dad looked at Mom quizzically and she said, "Children, there's no such thing as a dragon, but I do remember how much fun I had in that tree house with your

Uncle Richard! I am sure we can support you in building it again."

They all dug into the delicious dinner and dreamed about the project ahead.

Building the Fort

It was another hot and humid morning a few days after the planning for the fort. "Today is the day we will build the fort!" The children jumped out of bed, got dressed quickly, and dashed down to breakfast. As always their Mom had made their favorites. They gobbled down a huge pile of pancakes with lots of gooey syrup and gulped down big glasses of orange juice. They told their mom they would be busy all day building the fort and they would let their parents know if they needed help. Their Dad had taught them how to use the various tools. The supplies had been delivered the day before and he had used his power saw to cut the big pieces so they would be ready.

The three headed to the old oak tree. They knocked on the tree three times, the magic door opened, and they were off down the spiral staircase and up the yellow pathway to the dragon's cave. They burst into the cave and found the dragon busy reading his morning newspaper.

"Good morning and what are we planning to do today?"

"Today is the day to build the fort! Don't you remember?"

The dragon looked over his spectacles and smiled. "Ah yes, today is the day! How will you begin?"

The children reviewed all of their plans with the dragon and explained each step. They were ready to get started and they wanted the dragon to come and help. "We will need you to check us as we do each thing and to probably help with the lifting."

"At your service, children. This will be fun." The dragon bowed and the children giggled. Then they climbed aboard the dragon to fly down to the old oak tree.

Tom and Matt began to sort the wood into piles for each part of the project. Sara had a checklist and made sure everything was ready. She organized the tools and the bolts and nails so they could quickly build each piece. The dragon settled down under the tree to watch them work.

"OK, the first thing we need to do is put up the floor beams and joists. Get those brackets and nails and also those large screws." Everyone got their tools and then asked the dragon to lift the first piece as they climbed up to his head to begin work. If you had been passing by you would have seen a board floating in the air and three children flying around hammering and screwing the board in place on the tree because, of course, as an adult you wouldn't be able to see the dragon. But the children were safe on the dragon's head and back.

The project proceeded as each floor joist was put into place. Once the joists were secured the dragon checked to make sure they were safe. The children began to lay the floor boards. This was a lot of fun because they could now

see the fort grow beneath their feet. By lunch time, thanks to the dragon's help, the floor of the fort was completed. They took a break for lunch and went inside. Mom asked how things were going and the children were careful to not mention the dragon, but told her that they were making really good progress. Mom said she would come for a visit later in the afternoon to see.

After lunch the dragon lifted the boards for the walls up to the fort floor and the children got all four walls built. They realized when the dragon went home to his cave, they would not be able to get down, so it was time to build the ladder and the elevator hoist. The ladder was pretty easy and Tom got it put together in about half an hour. Sara and Matt worked on the elevator hoist. They had studied "dumb waiters" on the website for Monticello since Thomas Jefferson had used them, so they knew how to build the little elevator for carrying supplies up to the fort.

With the help of the dragon, Matt hung a large pulley on one of the branches. Then he guided a large rope through the pulley and down to Sara. She had built the wooden box that would be the elevator and tied the rope securely to the top of the box. It was not big enough for a person, but you could lift a lot of supplies up to the fort in it.

The children were all satisfied with their work when their Mom arrived to look at things. "Wow, you all have done a lot! Even a ladder and a dumb waiter! That is really cool! I remember Uncle Richard and I built a fort very similar to this one. We read a book about the Swiss Family Robinson and got our ideas from there."

The children looked at each other and then at the dragon. Why did Mom know about the Swiss Family

Robinson and why did this fort look so familiar to her? The dragon shrugged his shoulders as if to say he didn't know what she was talking about.

Mom climbed the ladder and Sara took her on a tour of their plans. She explained about the dumb waiter for supplies, the big window to look at the mountain, and the storage closet for all of their toys. As they moved through the fort, Sara's Mom had a funny look on her face. She touched each part as if she were trying to remember something. Sara asked, "Mom, are you all right?"

"Oh yes, dear. I am just trying to remember when I played here. So many memories I have forgotten. I see that you still need to do the roof and will you have a lookout on top? And where is the knot hole?"

Matt and Tom had joined them and Tom asked, "What knot hole?"

Mom searched the tree and pointed to a large knot hole from an old tree branch that been cut off. "There it is! I remember Richard and I always thought it was a magic mirror or something like that."

Matt asked Sara, "Did we plan to have a lookout?"

Mom said, "Well, we used to climb up on the roof to look out on the mountain, but I think Sara had a better idea to put this big window in the side of the fort. So you can look out at the mountain and also watch for your enemies!"

The children laughed to hear their Mom pretending with them about pirates and bad guys trying to get into the fort. She seemed to understand all the fun they had planned for this new fort. They decided they had done enough for one day and they would return tomorrow to finish the fort. They all climbed down and began to head for the house. Sara lingered behind and went over to talk with the dragon.

"Do you know why my Mom was acting so weird about this fort?"

"Well Sara, your mom was a child once upon a time and she did live here and she did have a tree fort, so I would guess she was trying to remember things from her childhood."

Sara was thinking there might be more to it. "Hmmmm! Well, thank you so much for your help today. It is such a good feeling to see something that we planned out really come together. It really is a cool fort, Mr. Dragon! Thanks!"

"It was a great pleasure, Sara. I'll see you all tomorrow to complete the fort." The dragon flew away to his cave and Sara headed inside.

She arrived in the kitchen just in time to hear her two brothers telling their mom how the dragon had helped with the building of the fort, and their Mom said, "Children, there's no such thing as a dragon. You worked really hard and I am proud of all that you did. I am sure you will finish tomorrow."

The Dragon's Library

It was the first Saturday in September after school began. The children jumped out of bed and ran to the window. It was raining and it looked like a day to be indoors. The children got dressed and raced down to breakfast. They ate piles of yummy pancakes with lots of gooey syrup and guzzled down their big glasses of orange juice, waved goodbye to Mom, and dashed out to the magic tree.

Sara knocked three times on the tree and the door opened. The children scurried down the spiral staircase to the yellow path and ran through the tunnel to the dragon's cave. The dragon was sitting in his rocking chair reading the morning newspaper. "Good morning, children! How does it feel to be back in school?"

"It's not so bad. It is great to see all of our friends again. And my teacher is really cool and nice! He's told us all about his travels this summer to Europe and California." Matt was in fourth grade.

"Yeah, my teacher is really nice too! She gave us new pencils and paper to do our work and she reads us a story every day after lunch so we can rest before we work in the afternoon." Tom was beginning second grade.

"And Sara, how is your new class?" asked the dragon.

"Well, it's great to see all of my friends, but they seem to be so concerned over what they are wearing and how they look. And now they are talking about all the boys in fifth grade. I think it is pretty silly so I am just enjoying the teacher's lessons and doing my work. We are going to learn some really cool math this year called algebra, so I am really excited about the year ahead."

"That sounds terrific, children! I am so glad things are starting out so well."

"But...,"Matt said, "we have to read 25 books this year!"

"And...,"Sara added, "we have to do all these research projects."

"And I have to learn how to write stories!" Tom added.

The dragon raised his eyebrows. "Perhaps I can help. Come visit my library. You may find that reading all those books, finding all that information, and finding good ideas to write about may be easier if you use my resources."

The children followed the dragon through the cave to the library. The room was beautiful and it was lit by glowing candles. There were hundreds of books. They recognized many of their favorite titles---The Cat in the Hat, Winnie the Pooh, Miss Nelson, Harry Potter, and so many others.

"But Mr. Dragon, these are books that we have already read."

"Oh, I think you will find them very interesting to read again. There's nothing wrong with reading a good book again. You can always enjoy them a second time. Why not pick one of your favorites?"

Tom pulled out <u>The Cat in the Hat</u>. "This was one of my favorites in first grade." As he opened the book, the Cat jumped out of the page to tell the story! As he turned each page, the story unfolded like a movie with little characters dancing across the pages. "This is great!"

Matt found his favorite Harry Potter and began to read and watch the story unfold. "This is really cool! It's like the magic is really real!"

Sara searched through all the familiar titles and found some her favorites, <u>Stuart Little</u>, <u>The Secret Garden</u>, and <u>Adventures with Grandpa Ek</u>.

All day long the children pulled down books and watched the stories unfold before their eyes. They had so much fun revisiting old friends in the stories. Then Tom found a special shelf that was up high and had a locked screen over it.

"Hey, Mr. Dragon, what are these books? Can I read one of them? Why are they locked up?"

The dragon came over and eyed the shelf. "These are the secret dragon magic books and they are only for dragons. They can be very dangerous if you don't know how to handle them. They are not for people."

"But Mr. Dragon, I could read one of them. I'm a good reader and I'm really smart. Then maybe I could do some magic!"

"No, you must understand that these books are not for people. They are only for dragons. You must leave this shelf alone."

"Oh, all right," Tom said. But he kept eyeing the shelf and trying to figure out how to get one of those books. But that's a story for another time.

Finally it was time to go home. The dragon waved his claw and all the books returned to the shelves on their own. The children squealed with excitement.

"Oh, Mr. Dragon, thank you so much! That was so much fun! Can we each take a book home?"

"I think that would be fine. You can each choose a book and bring it back next time you visit."

The children searched the shelves and they each picked out a book. "Thanks Mr. Dragon! We'll see you next Saturday." The children skipped down the yellow path to the spiral staircase with their books under their arms and up to the doorway in the tree. They raced into the kitchen with their books in hand.

Mom greeted them. "So, what have you all been up to today?"

The children showed her their books and talked about going to the library. Mom said, "That was a long walk to the library!"

The children all exclaimed, "Oh, Mom, we got these books from the dragon's library, not the public library! Look, when we open the books, they tell the stories to us." But when the children opened the books for their mom, no characters appeared since adults don't believe in dragons and can't see the magic.

And Mother said, "Children, there's no such thing as a dragon!"

A Dragon's Halloween

It was a beautiful Saturday morning in October and the fall leaves were just gorgeous. The children jumped out of bed and ran to the window. The hillside was glowing in the morning sunrise as the sun hit the golden leaves on the trees. Halloween was next week and it was time to visit the dragon to prepare for trick or treating and parties!

The children dressed quickly and dashed down to breakfast. Mom had made their favorites. They gobbled down a huge pile of pancakes with lots of gooey syrup and gulped down big glasses of orange juice. The children thanked their mom for a great breakfast and off they went to the big old tree in the backyard. Sara knocked on the tree three times and the secret door opened. The children ran inside and down the staircase to the yellow path. They raced up the path to the dragon's cave.

The dragon was sitting in his rocking chair enjoying his morning newspaper. "Ah, children! How good to see you! How was school this week? What great adventure shall we go on today?"

"Oh, Mr. Dragon, we spent this week getting ready for Halloween! We read books and tales about Halloween and then we studied all about how bad candy is for our teeth and then we did some math problems about how to make a witch's brew. And now we have to get ready for the big party on Monday. And then we get to go trick or treating!"

"Hmmmm," said the dragon. "I know what a party is because we dragons often have parties. But what is trick or treating?"

"Well, we get dressed up in costumes like pirates and clowns and monsters and stuff like that! Then we go from house to house knocking on the doors and saying 'Trick or Treat'. Then people give us candy and prizes. It is so much fun, especially going in the dark!"

"Really? And so what will your costumes look like?"

Sara was quick to reply, "I am going to be an ugly and powerful witch. I'll have a magic wand and if someone doesn't give me some candy I'll put a magic spell on them!"

And the boys chimed in, "We're going to be pirates. We'll have patches on our eyes and pirate hats and even pirate swords. We'll tell people to give us their treasure or else they'll walk the plank!"

"Sounds awfully violent to me. Do you really scare people like this?"

The children giggled. "No, Mr. Dragon! It is just for fun. Nobody gets hurt and it is just acting. But we have sooooo much fun sneaking around. Aren't you going to come with us?"

The dragon raised one eyebrow and asked what he could possibly be for Halloween. You probably remember that only children can see dragons, so he couldn't go as a dragon because no one would see him. Tom said, "Oh, we can make this really scary! You can wear a sheet like a ghost and fly us through the air! People will really freak out at that!"

The children giggled again and asked the dragon to please wear a big white sheet and fly like a ghost. He said he could do that and it would be a lot of fun. The children stayed in the cave for the rest of the day, planning their Halloween night of fun. Then they dashed home for dinner along the path, up the stairs, and into the kitchen. They were careful not to mention the dragon since they thought their Mother would not let them trick or treat with a dragon.

Halloween night came and the children got all dressed up and told their Mother they would be home by 8 pm and she said she would be watching for them and to be careful! They ran out to the street and shouted, "Mr. Dragon!" Suddenly a huge white sheet came flying through the night sky. The moon was shining and the sheet really looked like a ghost. The sheet landed next to the children. "How do I look?" the dragon asked. The children recognized the dragon's voice and they all had a good laugh.

They walked down the street knocking on each door, two pirates, a witch, and a very big ghost. Most of the adults were very impressed with their costumes and especially the big ghost. The children and dragon collected big bags of candy. As they approached an intersection, some older kids came over and told them to give them all of their candy. Sara, Tom, and Matt were scared but the big ghost flew over the older kids and told them in a loud voice, "I don't think you want to bother this witch! She is very powerful and could turn you into frogs!"

The older kids laughed and gave Sara a shove. Matt and Tom stepped forward to protect their sister and then she stood up and waved her magic wand at the kids and POOF, they turned into frogs! "Oh my goodness, did I do that?!" Sara exclaimed. Her brothers jumped back and stared at her.

The dragon chuckled under his sheet. "The spell is only temporary and it will wear off in a few hours. They will have plenty to talk about at school tomorrow. They will always remember how it felt to be small and slimy and that should cure them of their bullying ways."

The children and the dragon continued to trick or treat and after an hour they were really tired and the bags were heavy. The children climbed on the dragon's back and he flew them home. That Halloween night everyone saw a huge ghost flying through the sky with a witch and two pirates riding on its back. The next day at school everyone was talking about it. And the bullying kids were telling everyone about a powerful witch who turned them into frogs. Everyone thought they had eaten too much candy and the sugar went to their heads.

The dragon dropped the children off at their house and said good night. He flew off into the sky to his cave with his bag of candy. The children ran into the kitchen and showed their Mother their big bags of candy. They talked about all the costumes they had seen and all the decorations, and even one neighbor who had dressed up as a clown and told jokes. Then one of the brothers said, "And the dragon was a huge ghost and we got to ride on his back through the Halloween sky and we scared everybody!"

And Mother said, "Children, there's no such thing as a dragon." But the children had had the best Halloween ever!

Thanksgiving

It was Thanksgiving morning and the children awoke to savory smells from the preparation for the big feast later that day. They jumped out of bed and got dressed. They wanted to visit the dragon this morning to let him know about Thanksgiving and to invite him to dinner.

The children dashed down to breakfast. Mom had been busy cooking the pies and other dishes and preparing the turkey so the children had to have cereal. That was OK because the whole dinner would be a special meal for their family. The children thanked their mom for working so hard preparing the feast. They told her they would set the table when they got back from their morning adventure. They ran to the big old tree in the backyard and Matt knocked on the tree three times and the secret door opened. The children ran inside and down the staircase to the yellow path. They raced up the path to the dragon's cave.

The dragon was sitting in his rocking chair enjoying his morning newspaper. "Ah, children! How good to see you! How are you today?"

"Oh, Mr. Dragon, today is Thanksgiving and we are going to have a huge meal with all kinds of great food! And after we are stuffed full we will sit down and watch TV and fall asleep on the couch and just have a relaxing day with our family."

"Hmmmm," said the dragon. "That sounds delightful. What is Thanksgiving?"

"Well, this is an American holiday where we celebrate some of the first settlers who came to our country from England. The Pilgrims were a group of people who were persecuted in England because they wanted to have their own religion. They took the chance to be free and got on a little ship called the Mayflower and sailed to America. It was a long journey and about half of the Pilgrims died on the trip.

"When they landed here in Massachusetts, they built a little town called Plymouth. They were lucky the local Native Americans were kind and gave them food and helped them survive. It was really tough for a few years and then their colony began to grow and flourish. So the Pilgrims were some of the first colonists to start our new nation."

"So why the big party and why call it Thanksgiving?"

"Well, the Pilgrims decided to have a big party to thank the Indians for helping them survive. And that was how Thanksgiving got started. Now we celebrate the day to give thanks for everything we have, like our families and friends, our food, our health, and our freedom."

"Our Mom and Dad are preparing a big feast for our family. Our Uncle Richard and his family will come to dinner, too. So since you are a part of our family now, we wanted to invite you too and give thanks for your new friendship!"

The dragon smiled and thanked the children for including him. He asked where the party would be. They explained that it would be in the dining room and they were going home now to set the table.

"I will be glad to come, but remember the adults will not be able to see me, so don't set a place for me or tell them I am there. They will just get confused."

The children all agreed and told the dragon to come at 4 pm. They waved goodbye and ran up the path, climbed the stairs, and ran to the house to help with the feast.

Sara set the big dining room table for her family of 5 and Uncle Richard's family of 4. She placed the plates at each seat and then the silverware next to the plates. She folded napkins and set up decorations on the table, too. The table looked great!

Matt and Tom helped in the kitchen with all the different dishes. Matt peeled the potatoes and Tom washed the yams. They scrubbed the green beans and opened the cans of corn. They watched their parents prepare the huge turkey to go into the oven. By noon everything was cooking or ready to cook for the big dinner. Everyone collapsed on the couch for an hour to rest.

Then at 1:00 Mom roused everyone and reminded them Uncle Richard and family would arrive by 2:00 and everyone needed to get dressed. So they all got cleaned up and dressed for the party. Around 2 o'clock, a blue van pulled into the driveway and Richard's family came into the house. Everyone was busy talking and the children all went up to the playroom to have some fun. The adults finished up the preparations for the dinner.

At 4 pm Mother told the children to come down for dinner. They knew the table would be full of yummy food and they dashed down to their seats. As everyone settled into their chairs, there was a brief whoosh of wind and the dragon appeared in a corner of the dining room. Sara, Matt, and Tom winked and waved to the dragon and Richard's children stared at the dragon. Sara put her finger over her lips to tell them to be quiet and then said, "I'll explain later."

Of course, the adults could not see the dragon and they went right on with their conversations and eating. The children dug into the food as well and the dragon carefully helped himself to each tasty dish reaching over everyone. It was a wonderful meal with turkey and gravy, mashed potatoes, yams, corn, green beans, and lots of stuffing. For dessert they had pumpkin pie with lots of whipped cream.

By the end of dinner they were all stuffed, even the dragon! He had a silly grin on his face and licked his lips several times. He thanked the children and quietly slipped out of the dining room with another brief whoosh of air.

Uncle Richard's children could no longer contain themselves and they exclaimed, "Why was there a dragon at our Thanksgiving feast?!"

The adults all looked at them and Mother said, "Children, there's no such thing as a dragon. Maybe all this food just fed your imaginations!"

Everyone settled down in the living room for their Thanksgiving nap. Richard's children wanted to know more about the dragon and Sara took them upstairs to the playroom to explain it all.

Snow Day!

The children had fallen asleep last night hoping the weatherman knew what he was talking about. As they jumped out of bed in the morning, they were not disappointed. They stared out the window at a beautiful landscape of snow, about 15 inches deep. This meant that schools would be closed and they could enjoy the day with the dragon.

They raced down to breakfast where Mother informed them schools were indeed closed. They cheered and then sat down to their hearty breakfast of pancakes with lots of gooey syrup and a big glass of orange juice. They jumped up, thanked their mom, and dashed out to play in the snow. The snow was wet and easily packed down. They ran over to the magic tree and knocked three times and the door opened. They clambered down the stairway and up the yellow path into the dragon's cave.

"Well, good morning children! I thought you would be in school today!"

"Oh no, Mr. Dragon, we have a snow day!!"

"What is that?"

"Well, when it snows and the roads are dangerous and the schools can't shovel it fast enough and the school buses can't run and kids can't walk on the sidewalks, they have to close schools so no one gets hurt. So we have the day off and we can have some fun in the snow."

"I have heard of snow, but I really don't know much about it and I have never seen it."

"Well, come on! We'll show you all the great things you can do on a snow day!"

So the dragon put a scarf around his big neck, the children climbed on his back, and they flew out of the cave into the morning sunlight and the brilliant white snow. Everything was coated and as the dragon landed in the meadow, he slid across the field before he could bring himself to a stop.

"Oh my, children, snow is very slippery!"

The children giggled and explained to the dragon that snow was frozen water, so it was just like ice. They all talked at once about all the things they could do with snow.

"Whoa, slow down children. I can't even understand all of this. Let's begin with one thing and move on to others."

Sara stepped forward and said, "Let's begin with sledding down a hill!" The boys cheered and the dragon had a quizzical look.

"So what do we do?" he asked.

"Just watch!" the children exclaimed.

They climbed to the top of the little hill in the meadow. They found some big pieces of wood and one at a time they jumped onto the wood and slid down the hill. As they packed down the path, it got faster and faster. The dragon thought this looked like great fun and he gave it a try. Well, being such a big dragon, he slid down on his belly and made a huge pathway. When he reached the top of the hill again, the children climbed on his back and they slid down the hill faster and faster. After several trips down the little hill, the dragon had a new thought.

"If we can go this fast on a little hill, what can we do on the mountain?"

The children were a little worried about a big mountain, but they trusted the dragon, so off they all flew to the top of the mountain. The dragon surveyed the mountain and found a good pathway to the bottom. Everyone took a deep breath and off they went. The dragon was going faster and faster down the mountain and the children held on really tightly. They had never gone so fast! When they reached the bottom they all rolled into the snow laughing and screaming about how much fun that was! The dragon said, "Let's do it again!" And the group flew back to the top of the mountain several more times and enjoyed a fantastic sledding experience on the back of the dragon.

Sledding can get pretty tiring with all that screaming and holding on for dear life. So the group finally just took a break and everyone laid down in the snow. Tom and Matt started swinging their arms and legs and made snow angels. The dragon thought this was really cool so he did the same. His snow angel turned out to look more like a giant snow bird, but he was so pleased with what he had made.

Next the children wanted to make a snowman. They showed the dragon how to roll balls of snow and stack them to make the body. Then they collected sticks and stones to make the arms and the face. The dragon really liked this idea, so he made a snow dragon. Of course, because he is so big, his snow dragon was also very big---about 20 feet tall! The children could not believe their eyes. They had never seen such a big snowman. And the dragon used his sharp claws to carve the snow so that the snow dragon really looked like a dragon. After about an hour, the group had made almost a dozen snow men and dragons. The hill looked like a small army of snow people.

The dragon was having so much fun he decided to add a little magic to the scene. He waved his claw and the snow in front of the children turned blue. The dragon pointed at the blue snow and a huge snow fort rose out of the snow. It was two stories high and sparkled in the sunlight. It looked like a castle! The children were amazed and climbed into the blue snow fort and ran all over the fort.

Sara finally said that she was cold and tired. It was time to go back to the cave. But Matt picked up a piece of snow and threw it at her. She picked up another snowball and hit him square in the chest. This began the big snowball fight and everyone was wildly throwing snow at each other, hiding behind the walls of the blue fort. As the dragon got the hang of it, he would pick up bigger and bigger pieces of snow. When he finally buried all three children in a big pile, they all giggled and said it was time to go.

The children climbed onto the dragon's back and flew to the cave. They took off all of their snow clothes and hung them by the dragon's fireplace. The dragon brought out big mugs of hot chocolate and some yummy dragon cookies. Tom asked where the marshmallows were for the hot chocolate? His sister reminded him that it was not polite to ask for such things, but the dragon said he had plenty of marshmallows, so he got some from the kitchen. The group enjoyed the warm cocoa and cookies and talked about all the fun they had had in the snow. The dragon said, "I really like this snow day. What a great idea!"

It was finally time to head home, so the children got all their warm and dry snow clothes back on, waved goodbye to the dragon, and ran down the yellow path to the stairs. They climbed up and out and ran to the house. As they dashed into the house, Mother asked if they had enjoyed their snow day.

"Oh, Mom, it was great! We went sledding and built a bazillion snow people, and had a big snow fight! It was so much fun! And you know the dragon had never seen snow and he thought it was really great and he built a huge snow dragon about 20 feet tall!"

And Mother said, "Children, there's no such thing as a dragon!"

Dragon Flu

It was a beautiful but cold morning in February and the children jumped out of bed ready for a full day of fun with the dragon. They got dressed and raced down to breakfast. They gobbled down lots of pancakes covered in gooey syrup and a big glass of orange juice. As they waved goodbye to their Mother, Matt grabbed his new laptop computer to show the dragon.

The children dashed to the tree, knocked three times and the door opened. They slid down the spiral staircase and dashed up the yellow path to the dragon's cave. The big wooden door was shut and there was a sign on the door which said: "WARNING---DRAGON FLU! Quarantine!" The children drew back in fear for the dragon. Tom asked, "What does it mean, quarantine?"

"That means the dragon is sick and could make us sick! So we are not supposed to go into the cave."

Sara yelled at the door, "Mr. Dragon, are you in there?" There was no answer so the children pounded on the wooden door. They yelled together, "ARE YOU IN THERE?!"

There was a low groaning and growling sound and a weak voice said, "Go away children. I am very sick and I think I am dying. Go away."

Sara yelled again, "Can people get this dragon flu?"

The dragon responded in a whisper, "Only dragons. People are safe."

"Then we're coming in!" And the children opened the heavy door. They found the dragon sprawled on his couch. His beautiful green glowing skin was dull and more gray than green. His eyes were bloodshot and he had weird yellow spots on his hands and feet. His long tongue was hanging out of his mouth. He looked really sick!

He whispered again, "Oh, children. I am afraid that all the dragons have caught this flu. Even the dragon doctors are sick and they say it is a plague that will kill us all."

The children reacted with tears and cries of "Oh no!" But then they pulled themselves together and Sara said, "We are going to figure this out and make you better. Matt, get that computer going. Go to the website that diagnoses diseases."

Matt got the website running and entered all the symptoms. The result on the screen said: NO such disease exists. "That can't be! This website knows every disease!"

Tom said, "Wait a minute. The dragon isn't human, he is a reptile. Go to a veterinarian website for reptile diseases. Put the symptoms into that website."

Matt found a reptilian veterinarian website and entered the symptoms. A reptilian flu came up on the screen. The diagnosis was yellow spotted foot and hand flu and unfortunately the website said it could not be cured. Very few reptiles had ever survived it.

Sara turned to the dragon. "We know what you have, but we can't find a cure. You once told me about a secret medical book of magic that you have in the library. May I get it?"

The dragon opened one eye and stared at Sara. "This is the end, so I don't see any reason why you can't look at the magic. It will all vanish as we do. Go to the top shelf and find the orange covered book. Do not touch any of the other books. You will need this key." The dragon pointed to his neck and then he fainted.

Sara ran to the dragon's library. She pulled a chair over to the shelf and found the book. She saw a lot of other interesting books including the dragon's diary, but she followed orders and did not touch any of them. She brought the book to the dragon. He opened his eye again. "Dragons are strictly forbidden to share these magic secrets with humans, but I fear that if you don't find a cure, we shall all perish. Do your best, Sara." The dragon touched the cover with his claw and it magically opened. And the dragon fainted again.

Sara searched the index and found yellow spotted foot and hand flu. The description was exactly the same as what the dragon had and there was a magical cure listed on the page! Sara patted the dragon and he opened his eye again. "There is a cure but it requires some weird stuff and an 'orb'. What is that?"

The dragon whispered, "You will find the ingredients in the kitchen cabinet. The orb is a round crystal in a chest in my bedroom. It is the source of my magical powers. Use the same key to open the chest." And the dragon fainted again.

"All right, guys! Let's get busy saving our dragon!" The brothers took the list of ingredients to the kitchen and began collecting all the weird things needed for the cure. They piled everything on the kitchen table and found a big mixing bowl to make the potion.

While they collected the ingredients, Sara went to the dragon's bedroom with the key. She found the chest on the nightstand next to the dragon's bed. She unlocked the chest and found a beautiful glowing green crystal. It was a perfect sphere. As she carefully picked it up, she could feel the power of the crystal on her skin. She walked slowly to the kitchen and placed the sphere on the table on a towel so it would not roll away.

Tom read the procedures as Sara and Matt measured and poured each ingredient into the bowl. They knew that following the recipe exactly would save the dragon. First they had to grind up the dry ingredients. Dried bat wings and spider webs went into the bowl, then some potato chips and red pepper. Matt ground them together. Next they added two cups of dragon's tears from a big jar, one cup of orange juice, and four cups of water from the Sargasso Sea. "Why does the dragon have all of this weird stuff?"

"He uses it to keep the dragons healthy and safe. But it is a pretty strange mixture!"

Tom used a whisk to mix all the powders and liquids together. It had a strange color, but it smelled a lot like their favorite breakfast of pancakes and orange juice.

"The last ingredients are fresh mint and daisies! Go to the garden and get them now!" The boys climbed out the cave entrance and went along the cliff pathway to the garden. They picked the mint and the flowers and carefully found their way back to the cave.

Sara was sitting by the dragon petting his head and telling him to hold on. "The recipe says to crush six daisies into the potion and squeeze in some mint juice. Hurry up!"

The boys completed the potion and it began to smoke and bubble. "The recipe says that when the smoke turns blue you must drop the orb into the potion." The boys were mesmerized by the bubbling and they were not moving. Sara jumped to her feet, grabbed the orb, and as the smoke turned blue, she slid the crystal into the potion. "You must count to ten and then pull the orb out."

Tom had started counting to ten. Matt told his sister, "You put it in there so you can pull it out." As he reached ten, Sara put her hand into the potion and pulled the orb out. It burned her hand, but she had to do it to save the dragon. She placed the orb on the towel and ran to the sink to rinse her hand.

Matt read the last step. "You must give the potion to the dragon in a golden cup. Where are we going to find a golden cup?" The children searched the cave for any kind of cup. Tom found a golden cup, but it was a trophy of a girl playing soccer. It was engraved with the words, "Forever Friends".

"A trophy will have to do! We can't wait any longer. Fill the cup with the potion."

"But wait!" Matt said. "There is something scribbled in the margin of the book. It says something about repeating over and over, 'Heal my mighty dragon!' I guess we have to chant that as he drinks the potion."

The children ran to the dragon. He was very weak and his skin was almost black. Sara pried his large jaw open and she was careful to avoid his poisonous fangs. Matt poured the potion into the dragon's mouth as Tom chanted over and over, "Heal my mighty dragon!" As the cup was emptied, Matt and Sara joined the chant. After a while, nothing was happening and the children stopped chanting. They cried softly over the dragon fearing that he was lost. Their tears dripped on his skin and into his eyes.

Suddenly the dragon's skin began to glow and gradually he regained his color. He opened his eyes and he began to look more like their dragon. He was getting better!

It took more than an hour for the dragon to fully recover. Finally he shook his big head and said, "This is a miracle, children! You have saved me from the flu! I must now save the others! You have done a great service to the dragons and we will always owe you a great debt. It is time for you all to head home. I will work through the night to save each of the dragons with the potion you have prepared."

The children all hugged the dragon and said how glad they were he was better. They returned home exhausted. They told their Mother all about what had happened. Of course, Mother responded by saying, "There's no such thing as a dragon."

But Sara noticed a funny look on her mother's face as she stared out the window at the mountain. It was as if she was trying to remember something from long ago. "Mom, are you OK?"

"Oh yes, dear. I was just trying to remember what I had done with my old soccer trophy from when I was little. It was engraved with that saying you mentioned, 'Forever friends'. I wonder where it is?"

Discovery!

It was one of those rainy Saturdays in the spring when you couldn't play outside. The children looked out the window and knew it was a day to visit with the dragon. They got dressed, ran down to their favorite breakfast of pancakes, gooey syrup, and orange juice, waved goodbye to Mother, and dashed out to the magic tree. They knocked three times on the tree and the door opened. They rushed inside, up the yellow path, and into the dragon's cave.

The dragon was reading his morning paper in his rocking chair. "Good morning, children. How are you today?"

The children all talked at once about school and soccer and dance class and their school field trips. The dragon gave out a gentle laugh and thanked them for the updates. "What shall we do today?"

They all looked out the cave entrance and the rain continued to pour down. "Not a good day to go outside on an adventure, Mr. Dragon."

"Ah yes, a good day to read an adventurous book!" The children cheered for they knew this meant they would visit the dragon's library. The room was lined with beautiful wooden bookcases all the way to the ceiling. The chairs were comfy with big reading lamps. The children loved the dragon's books because when they opened the books, the story would come to life as they read. Little figures would appear and act out the story.

Matt found some adventure books about cowboys in the old west. Tom found a book called <u>The Adventures of Tom Sawyer and Huck Finn</u>. That sounded interesting. As the boys settled into their chairs, the dragon took Sara to a special shelf in the library.

"You will remember you are not to read the books on the top shelf. They are the special magic books that only dragons can read. But this shelf has my personal diaries and it is time for you to know more about my past. I think you will find this volume particularly interesting."

The dragon handed Sara a bright turquoise book and she settled down to read it. Each entry in this book was about a brother and sister and their adventures with a dragon. This was not about her and her brothers, but these children seemed to live in the same house where Sara and her brothers lived. Sara knew their house had been in her family for several generations so she was very confused and interested in reading this book.

As Sara snuggled into one of the big soft chairs, she skimmed through the book and found a story about "The Big Rescue". The boy and girl had come to the dragon's cave and could not find the dragon. There was a note and a map.

As the children followed the directions in the note they climbed out of the dragon's cave on a narrow path on the cliff. Sara had been on that path and knew it led to the dragon's garden! The children found a rope ladder hanging in the garden from the clouds and they climbed it in search of the dragon. At the top they came into a cave much larger than the dragon's cave.

As their eyes adjusted to the dark, they saw the dragon locked in a cage in the middle of the cave. The brother and sister ran to the dragon and asked what was going on.

"Oh children! Be careful! As I was wandering through the forest looking for those blue berries I like so much, I stepped on a bush and was suddenly swept up into a giant net! Then this large troll came along and picked me up in the net and carried me to this cave. He threw me into this cage and said something about dinner!"

The brother said, "This makes no sense Mr. Dragon. Why don't you just use your magic powers on the troll and escape?"

"That's the problem, children. My magic will not work on a troll and they have special powers that I cannot overcome."

The sister said, "So we will have to solve this the old-fashioned way."

The children heard the troll coming into the cave and scurried to a hiding place. The troll was huge, over 30 feet tall, twice as big as the dragon. He had a large red nose, crooked yellow teeth, and scraggly hair. He squinted a lot and he smelled terrible. He seemed to be very angry, moaning and groaning.

"Hey little dragon! You will be a tasty dinner for me tonight! I will get a big pot of water boiling so I can make my famous dragon stew!" And he let out an awful laugh that echoed through the cave. The children could tell the dragon was frightened of the troll.

The children saw a large pot on the troll's gas stove. It was beginning to warm up and bubble. As the troll lumbered away, the brother went to the stove and turned it off. The water stopped boiling. When the troll returned he found the stove turned off. He scratched his head and said, "Huh? I thought I turned this on." He switched the stove back on, checked the flame, and lumbered off. The boy turned the stove off again.

This scenario repeated itself several times over the next hour while the sister tried to open the cage. The only way to get the dragon out was to get the troll's key that was hanging on his belt. The children had to find a way to get the troll to lean down so they could reach the key.

The troll was not very smart, but he began to realize the stove flame kept going out. So he knelt down to look under the stove. The girl realized that this was her chance and she dashed out of hiding to grab the key. She unhooked the key from the belt just as the troll stood up. Just in time! The troll stayed by the stove to watch the water boil. This was a problem.

The children tiptoed to the cage with the key and carefully placed it in the lock. Then the brother yelled down the cave as loud as he could. His voice echoed deep into the cave and the troll looked up. "What was that?!" He clomped down into the cave to find the source of the noise.

The children quickly turned the key and the dragon was able to push open the heavy gate. The three ran out of the troll's cave and once in the sunlight the dragon spread his wings, and the children climbed aboard and off they flew. The troll came to the entrance of his cave and started bellowing at them. He grabbed large rocks and threw them with all of his might, but the dragon was a swift and accurate flier and avoided the rocks as they disappeared into the clouds.

When they reached the dragon's cave, they glided into the entrance. The dragon thanked the children over and over and praised them for their bravery. He brought out his favorite chocolate chip cookies that were only for special occasions and they all enjoyed a yummy snack of cookies and milk. The children asked the dragon how he could be safe from the troll.

The dragon explained that the troll could not come into the dragon's territory because of his magic. But the dragon could not resist the blue berries and he had crossed over into the troll's territory. The dragon had learned his lesson and he would not be going over there again. He would find those blue berries on his own land.

Sara continued to read to the end of the story realizing the last chapter was about the brother and sister growing up and having their own families. The sister moved into the white farmhouse, her family's traditional home. She had 3 children, a girl and two boys. Her name was Marie.

Sara stopped reading and her eyes grew large. "This story was about my Mother and my uncle Richard!" How could this be when her Mother always said there were no such things as dragons? Mother knew there were dragons! She had met their dragon when she was young.

Sara closed the book with a lot of questions for her Mother. The boys finished their books and the three children returned home along the yellow path, up the spiral staircase, and out of the tree. They burst into the kitchen and the brothers told their Mother all about the great stories they had read in the dragon's cave.

And their Mother said, "Boys, there's no such thing as a dragon." But Sara knew more about her Mother. She had a lot of questions that needed answers and they would talk another time.

The Nasty Little Dragon

It was a beautiful Saturday morning in May. The children jumped out of bed and ran to the window. The sun was shining brightly and the air smelled so sweet and clean. The children got dressed and raced down to breakfast. They ate piles of yummy pancakes with lots of gooey syrup and guzzled down their big glasses of orange juice, waved goodbye to Mother, and dashed out to the magic tree.

Tom knocked three times on the tree and the door opened. The children scurried down the spiral staircase to the yellow path and ran through the tunnel to the dragon's cave. The dragon was sitting in his rocking chair reading the morning newspaper. "Good morning, children! How are you today?"

"We are just great! It is a beautiful spring day and we want to go out and have some fun! Do you have any ideas where we could go?"

"On such a nice day, I think we could visit the forest, don't you?"

The children loved the forest. It was always so mysterious and full of surprises. But they always felt safe with the dragon. Once they had gone into the woods and another big orange dragon had chased them. Their dragon rose up and waved his magic claw and the orange dragon just vanished. They were always safe with their dragon.

"Yes, let's go there!"

The dragon made some peanut butter and jelly sandwiches for lunch and took a large jug of dragon juice and put everything into a backpack. Sara offered to carry the backpack and the dragon gave it to her. The children climbed aboard the dragon's back and they flew out of the cave.

It was a gorgeous spring day and they could see for miles. The sky was blue and full of white puffy clouds. The dragon swooped through the clouds and the children saw the forest below. As they landed in a clearing, Matt asked the dragon if the forest had a name. The dragon replied, "I'm not sure the forest has an official name. What would you like to call it?"

Sara said that 'Emerald Forest' sounded good to her and Matt voted for the "Magic Forest". Tom said, "How about we call it the 'Mysterious Forest' since we never know what mysterious adventure we will find?" They all agreed on the Mysterious Forest.

The dragon pronounced, "Forever more this forest will be known as the Mysterious Forest." And he waved his claw and pixie dust flew through the trees.

The group began to hike down a pathway deep into the darkness of the forest. It was cool and smelled so fresh. Everyone was enjoying the hike. They saw all kinds of birds and some very strange looking animals, too. They came to a stream where the water was brilliant green and bubbled and flowed among big rocks. "Let's eat lunch!" they shouted.

Sara opened the backpack and passed out the sandwiches and the dragon opened the jug of dragon juice for all to share. As they began to eat, they heard a strange howling noise from off in the forest. Everyone turned to see where the sound was coming from. They heard a strange zip zap sound and turned back to find that each of their sandwiches had a big bite taken out of it.

"Hmmm," said the dragon. "Something is not quite right here!"

Then they heard some strange screaming from another direction and they all looked that way. They heard the zip zap again and found more of their sandwiches gone.

The dragon told the children that regardless of whatever was making that noise, they should keep their eyes on their sandwiches and finish eating them quickly. Even though there were more strange sounds, they all finished their food and drink keeping their eyes glued to their sandwiches. They fed some of the bread to some funny looking orange fish in the green stream and then they jumped from rock to rock. They did not hear any more noises or that zip zap sound.

After a while Sara stood up and put the backpack on her back and said, "Mr. Dragon, that was a delicious lunch and this has been great fun, but I think it is time to go back to the cave. Shall we go?"

The dragon looked about suspiciously, listening for more of the strange noises. He did not hear anything else and he agreed it was time to go. The children climbed aboard the dragon's back and off they flew to the cave. After their big day in the forest, the children were tired and plopped down onto the dragon's sofa. Sara dropped the backpack to the floor. There was a loud yelp from the backpack! Everyone jumped back.

The dragon stepped over to the backpack and eyed it carefully. "It appears we have picked up a passenger while we were in the forest. Whatever is in this backpack better speak up quickly before I squash you flat!"

As the dragon raised his giant foot, something flew out of the bag at an incredible speed and darted around the cave. "Well, children, I think we have brought home a bug! I'll get the flyswatter."

The strange creature flew about the cave banging into things and knocking over many of the dragon's belongings. First a lamp crashed to the floor, then a big vase began to fall and one of the boys caught it just in time. Next the strange thing darted across the room to the kitchen and the children heard pots and pans banging about. The dragon returned with the flyswatter. "Ah, the bug is in the kitchen. Let's get it."

As the group rounded the corner, they saw a tiny little dragon sitting on the counter gobbling down crackers. Mr. Dragon was really angry. "What do you think you are doing?!"

The tiny dragon grimaced and flew right into Mr. Dragon's eye and punched him in the nose. This made Mr. Dragon really mad and he tried to swat the little dragon. The little dragon let out an evil laugh and continued to fly about the kitchen knocking over things and hitting the big dragon. Suddenly he found himself inside a jar with the lid on tight. One of the boys had captured him.

The tiny dragon was very angry and banged against the jar. It was then that Matt realized the little dragon was covered in peanut butter and jelly. "So, you are the one who ate our sandwiches!"

The tiny dragon tried to sound big and scary and he puffed out his chest and spit out a little bit of fire. He said, "I was hungry and you had plenty and I decided to take your food."

Mr. Dragon grabbed the jar and was ready to throw it out of the cave, but Tom said, "No, Mr. Dragon! Let's see if we can help him."

So the dragon put the jar down on the table. Tom began to talk to the tiny dragon. "You know, you can't just go around stealing other people's food. That isn't right and you can get punished for that. Mr. Dragon was ready to squash you and throw you out the window."

"I don't care. I haven't eaten anything in a week and I was hungry and mad."

"I think I have this figured out!" Sara exclaimed. "I bet that whenever you are hungry you have a big temper. But once you get something to eat, you settle down and can be a lot nicer?"

The tiny dragon began to cry, but the big dragon wasn't so sure if this little dragon could be trusted. Matt opened the jar lid just enough to drop several cookies into the jar. The tiny dragon gobbled them down. "This poor little thing is starving. If we feed him, I think he will behave." Sara pointed at Tom and explained that he was very grumpy when he didn't get anything to eat. So the children fed the little dragon lots of food until he was stuffed. Then they poured him out of the jar onto the counter. He smiled and sat down on the counter.

"There, you see. He can be civil when he has been fed."

Mr. Dragon wasn't so sure and he scooped up the tiny dragon and put him into a small cage. The tiny dragon didn't even complain. "I don't want this little dragon in my cave. I think he is trouble just waiting to happen. I am going to put him back in the Mysterious Forest."

The Nasty Little Dragon sat up in his cage and eyed Sara and her brothers. "Wait a minute. Aren't you the children who found the cure for the Dragon Flu and saved all the dragons?"

"Well, yes, we did help to cure our dragon and then he cured all the rest."

"I've been wondering just how some children could do that?" the little dragon asked.

Tom explained about the potion and the magic orb and the chant and how the children had worked together to save their dragon. He told all about the magic book and finding the dragon's magic orb on the bedside table.

The Nasty Little Dragon listened carefully and he seemed to accept their explanation, but Mr. Dragon was not so sure about what the little dragon was up to. He didn't trust the little dragon and he couldn't wait to drop him back in the Mysterious Forest. "I'm going to take him back to the forest right after you all leave."

Sara agreed since she didn't understand dragon ways and she put together a large box of food for the tiny dragon. "Whenever you start to get angry, be sure to eat something. This will get you started, but you will have to find ways to get food. How do dragons find food?" Mr. Dragon said he would be sure to teach the tiny dragon how to find food and he would explain this to the children another time. They needed to go home and he would deliver the little creature back to the forest.

The children waved goodbye to the dragon and thanked him for a great day. They ran back up the yellow pathway, up the spiral staircase, and out of the door in the tree. They dashed into the kitchen just in time for dinner. Mother asked, "What have you all been up to today?"

The children began to tell her all about the Mysterious Forest and the strange noises and something eating their lunch and how one of the boys caught a tiny dragon in a jar and the big dragon didn't like him and....

Mother raised her hand and said, "Children, it's time for dinner and you know perfectly well that there's no such thing as a dragon!"

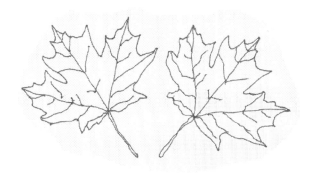

A New October

It was a beautiful Saturday morning in October, but things were different now. A year had passed and Sara was now in middle school. Between her schoolwork, her sports, and having fun with all of her friends, she did not have much time to play with her younger brothers anymore . This morning she awoke at her neighbor's house after enjoying a night of fun at her best friend's slumber party. The girls had been up late watching videos and telling stories. Sara had finally drifted off to sleep around 3 am. They were all asleep now in their sleeping bags all over the family room floor.

Sara stretched and rubbed her eyes and stared at the mountain out the back window. She imagined her brothers were already at the dragon's cave dreaming up some new adventure, but she was busy having a good time with her friends who were all fast asleep right now. Sara remembered all the fun she had had at the cave and all their travels with the dragon.

Suddenly there was a loud thump on the window and Sara saw a large paper airplane slide down the glass. That was very odd she thought and she slipped out of her sleeping bag and tiptoed outside to see what was going on. She found a paper airplane that was about three feet long.

As she unfolded the plane she found a simple message: "HELP! The Cave!" Sara recognized Tom's messy handwriting right away and knew something wasn't right. She quietly went back into the family room, wrote a quick thank you note to her friend, stuffed all of her things into her sleeping bag, and left the group fast asleep.

She ran across the yard to her house and burst into the kitchen. Her mother was busy cleaning. They had talked about the dragon after Sara had discovered the truth about her mother in the dragon's diary. Her mother vaguely remembered something about all of this from her childhood, but she had always thought it was a dream. And now it appeared that maybe it was not.

Sara's Mother was surprised to see her so early. "What's up, Sara? Did you all wake up this early?"

"Mom, something is very wrong! Where are the boys?" Her mom said the boys had eaten breakfast and gone out to play about an hour ago. They had gone up by the big oak tree and then disappeared. "So they went to see the dragon."

Sara's mom nodded her head. "I think that is the way, isn't it, Sara?"

"Mom, we need to go now." Sara showed her mom the paper airplane with the message. She explained how it had arrived and that this must be serious. They needed to rescue the boys at the cave.

"But Sara, I can't fit through that door in the tree."

"I know. It has been harder and harder for me to get through it. Last time I got stuck and the boys had to pull me through it. We need to try, Mom. Something is very wrong."

They ran out to the tree together and Sara knocked three times on the tree. The door opened, but it was clear that neither of them could fit through it any longer. Sara thought back to when they built the tree fort above their heads. "Mom, when we built the tree fort, the dragon said there was an emergency porthole we could use if we ever really needed to get to the cave. We need to climb up into the tree fort and find it."

Sara and her mother climbed up the rope ladder into the fort. The boys were not very good housekeepers and the tree fort was going to need a good cleaning later, but right now they had to find the porthole. "The dragon never told us where the porthole actually was! How are we going to figure this one out?"

Mother looked across the fort and had a brief memory of long ago. "It's the knot hole right over there. The one that I thought was a magic mirror. You put your hand on it and say something three times. Then something really amazing happens but I can't remember what." They crossed the tree fort to the knot hole. Sara put her hand on the knot hole. "Dragon, dragon, dragon!" Nothing happened. "Cave, cave, cave!" Still nothing. She continued saying any word she could think of three times. She turned to her Mother. "What do I need to say, Mom? You've got to remember!"

Mother searched her memory and remembered the day when she and her brother Richard had to do this to rescue the dragon. She had climbed into the fort, found the knot hole, placed her hand on the hole, and said? "Oh my, what was it?" Then she suddenly remembered. "I believe in dragons! Sara, say that three times. I believe in dragons!"

Mother put her hand on Sara's shoulder to reassure her as Sara said three times, "I believe in dragons, I believe in dragons, I believe in dragons!" The knot hole glowed yellow and Sara and her mom were sucked into a wind tunnel through the knot hole. It was both scary and exhilarating as they whooshed through the tunnel and landed at the entrance to the dragon's cave. The door was shut and locked.

Sara's mother was amazed. She had not been here in many years and all kinds of memories were flooding into her head. Sara turned to her and said, "Why didn't you tell me about that wind tunnel? That was really scary!"

"That's why! I knew you had to do it and if I told you what would happen, you would never try. Sometimes you just have to trust, Sara."

Sara tried to open the door, but it would not budge. She thought for a moment and remembered that the dragon hid a key under the doormat. She flipped the mat, retrieved the key, and opened the door. As they entered they felt a cold wind. The cave was dark and quiet. It was never like this. Even when the dragon had been captured by the troll, the cave was still warm and lighted. Now the cave was a mess. Furniture had been knocked over, drawers were emptied on the floor, papers were everywhere, and there had clearly been some kind of a struggle. This was really creepy.

Sara found a lantern and lit the wick. There was enough light to search through the cave. For her mom, every step was a trip back in time to her childhood. She had enjoyed so many adventures here and the dragon's love and spirit had always been with her all these years. She was thankful the dragon had returned to share his secrets with her children. But where were the boys?

Sara called Mother to the cave entrance. "Mom, what does this mean?" She had found a backpack and a map. There were three things in the backpack---a peanut butter and jelly sandwich, a mirror, and something that looked like one of the dragon's claws. Weird things for a rescue! The map showed a pathway through several mountain passes to a temple. Sara knew there weren't any mountains like that around here and certainly no temple on a mountaintop. "Mom, what does this mean?!"

Sara's Mother studied the map. She had seen this before. The dragon had warned her to never go to this temple without the backpack and the three items. They would protect her but she had to be careful. Mother explained as much as she could remember to Sara and told her to get on her way. "Remember, Sara, to use all the knowledge the dragon has taught you. The dragon's lessons are tools to help you in a crisis. Be careful and be safe. I will be with you in spirit."

Sara stared at her mother. "Aren't you coming too? I can't do this alone!"

"No, this is a journey only you can make. Grown-ups do not go to this place, and for children it can be very dangerous. You must follow the map exactly and use the three items in the backpack. The dragon and the boys have been captured and they are in great danger. When you reach the temple, you will know what to do. Sara, be careful and bring Matthew and Thomas back!"

Sara studied the map and began her climb on the narrow path to the top of the cliff. When she reached the vegetable garden she turned left down a path she had never seen before. Soon she reached the giant boulder where the children had first found the dragon so many years ago during a huge thunderstorm. As she rounded the boulder, the clearing was filled with fog. Somehow she knew she had to pass through the fog, so she took a deep breath and walked into the fog. She could only see the pathway at her feet and slowly stepped forward. After about 10 steps the fog cleared and she found herself on a very narrow bridge crossing a deep valley. She had somehow passed into another place not on the mountain, and she could already tell this was not safe. The bridge was only about 3 feet wide and if she stepped the wrong way she would fall thousands of feet into darkness. She focused on crossing the bridge and moved forward. It was only about a hundred steps to the end of the bridge, but the trip seemed to take hours. Sara finally reached the other end and rested.

What was she supposed to do with these three things in the backpack? While she really liked peanut butter and jelly sandwiches, she was sure that it was not for her. The mirror was only about the size of a book. What could you do with that? And the funny shaped object that looked like one of the dragon's claws, what could that be for? She guessed that when the time came, she would know what to do with each of them. She studied the map.

Sara was now in the land of the high mountains. She could see the pathway leading to the mountain pass about a mile ahead. She began to climb the rocky path. She was glad she had remembered to put on her sneakers and that she had grabbed a water bottle before they ran out of the kitchen at home. She took a sip of water as she walked.

Sara thought back to all the adventures they had had with the dragon. There were so many fun times in the Mysterious Forest, the days of playing games and reading those 3-D books, and cooking in the dragon's magical kitchen. And there had been some rescues, too. But it always seemed she knew the rescue would work out and the dragon would be there to protect them. He had taught them to be kind, to enjoy each day, and to be resourceful. They had to think their way through so many problems and she was confident every day thanks to the dragon's lessons.

She was so deep in her thoughts as she walked that she did not realize she had reached a huge gate. It was more than 20 feet tall built into the cliffs. She did not see any way around it. There was no doorknob or keyhole, nothing to suggest how to open it. So she decided to knock on the door and see what would happen. She picked up a rock and pounded on the door. She heard a moaning sound with a bit of a growl to it and then heavy footsteps approaching the gate. She ran and hid behind a big rock.

The gate opened and a big hairy monstrous thing that looked a lot like a bear peered out. It stood up on its hind legs and looked in every direction. It sniffed the air and growled some more. Sara did not like the look of the big teeth dripping with saliva and the glaring red eyes of this monster. It reared up once more and roared again and slammed the gate shut. Sara thought about how to get around this beast. Would the mirror or the sandwich help? She studied the situation and realized she could use the mirror and the sunlight to distract the beast.

Sara pounded on the gate again and as the beast came out, she used the mirror to shine light far down the path. The beast saw the dancing light and ran down the path growling. She quickly passed through the gate and entered a large green meadow. She ran to a nearby tree and hid. The beast returned, closed the gate, and lumbered off into the meadow. When it was gone, Sara studied the map and the field. She could see that the path led across the meadow to another group of mountains. At the top of one of the mountains she saw the temple.

She ran along the path through the meadow certain she could reach the temple quickly. The air was warm and it felt more like spring than the cold from the mountain path. At the end of the meadow she reached another gate. How could she open this one? Sara studied the gate and saw a strange keyhole. She took out the dragon claw and pushed it into the keyhole. Slowly she poked around until the lock clicked and the gate swung open. Thank goodness for the claw.

Sara walked into another clearing in the dark woods. She found a rope hanging from the cliff right below the temple. She began the long climb. At the top she found herself at the entrance to the temple. The doorway was glowing with lights and there were two dragon guards. As she approached they rose up and glared at her. Then they recognized the girl who had saved their lives from the dragon flu, they bowed, and let her pass into the temple.

As she moved down a long hallway she could hear many voices shouting in the light ahead. It sounded like a heated argument. Sara entered a large room in the middle of the temple. The ceiling seemed to go up forever into the sky. She snuck into the back of the room and saw Mr. Dragon and her brothers locked in a cage. They looked tired and the dragon was that same bluish color she remembered from the first time she saw the dragon on the mountain in the storm. This did not look good.

There were several dragons sitting together in a large box, a dragon up in front at a table, and two dragons pacing back and forth yelling at each other. One of the dragons was the nasty little dragon! He was carrying the dragon's magic orb! How did the nasty little dragon escape from his cage and why did he have the orb?

The nasty little dragon yelled over the other dragon, "I am telling the judge and the jury that this dragon has told humans about his magic orb and he has even let them use it! That is strictly forbidden! This dragon has violated our most sacred rule!"

The second dragon defended Mr. Dragon by saying, "And I am saying that the children learned about the orb on their own when they saved us all from the terrible dragon flu!

The Master Dragon would never foolishly give away our magic! He was unconscious! What is wrong with you? They saved your life!"

"Those children kept me locked up in a cage!"

"They fed you and kept you safe from your own destructive behavior! This court should be deciding to lock you up and not the Master Dragon!"

Sara remembered how they had captured the nasty little dragon and found out he was always hungry. As long as they kept feeding him, he was pretty calm and even friendly. She also recalled how all the dragons had gotten sick with some terrible flu and the children used the dragon's magic books and his orb to find a cure. And she was surprised to learn that their dragon was the Master Dragon, the king of all of the dragons.

Sara thought carefully about how to handle this situation. The dragon had always told her to use respect, self-control, and what she had learned. How could she use these now?

The dragons in the jury were mumbling to each other and the judge hit the table with a large hammer. "Silence! Everyone in my court will follow the rules. What evidence do you have to support your accusations?"

The nasty little dragon continued to argue and he got more and more agitated. He was losing his temper and would not let go of the orb which gave him power over the court. This was a big problem. With the orb's magic he could turn all the dragons against the Master Dragon!

Sara dug in her backpack and found the peanut butter and jelly sandwich. She stepped forward into the courtroom and placed the big sandwich on the nasty dragon's table as she approached the judge.

"A thousand pardons your honor for interrupting this important meeting," she said. All the dragons gasped as they recognized the girl who had saved them from the deadly flu. Even the judge calmed down and looked at her.

The nasty little dragon smelled something really good and looked around at his table. "A sandwich!" he exclaimed. "Your honor, this little girl is a spoiled brat!" and then he ran across the table. As he grabbed the sandwich he put the orb down on the table. Sara grabbed the orb and moved towards the cage without the nasty little dragon even noticing.

"I have come to this hallowed hall today to pay my respects to all the grand dragons," Sara said. She handed the orb through the bars of the cage to her brothers who ran to the dragon and gave it to him. He began to glow in his familiar powerful green color.

"It has been my honor to visit the Master Dragon and learn from him about the good and right way that a dragon should live. We humans have much to learn from your wisdom." At these compliments the dragons were all smiling and nodding their heads in approval.

Sara eloquently reminded the dragons that they had saved themselves through their magic spell and orb. She and her brothers were learning from the dragons and they were only instruments of the dragons. The children meant no disrespect of the sacred orb and they returned it to the Master Dragon as soon as he was better. All the dragons cheered and shouted, "Free the Master!" Hearing these words, the judge agreed and ordered that the Master Dragon and the boys be released.

The nasty little dragon had finished the sandwich and he began yelling at the judge calling him names and insulting the judge. "For your disrespect of this court, you nasty little dragon, you are sentenced to be caged. Put him in the cage now!" Guards seized the nasty little dragon and put him in the cage with a magic lock that could only be opened by the Master Dragon.

All was right again in the dragon kingdom and Sara had saved the day with her self-control, respect, and quick thinking. She had learned a lot from the Master Dragon and it had paid off.

The children and the dragon said goodbye to the court and walked out of the temple into the sunlight. The dragon spread his wings and they climbed aboard and they flew back to the dragon's cave. As they entered the cave, the children all said how sorry they were about the messed up cave. But then they found the cave was all back in order, the fire was blazing, and something smelled really good! Chocolate chip cookies! All was right in the cave again, but why?

Then Mother stepped out of the kitchen and welcomed them all back from their great adventure. The dragon smiled and she gave him a big hug. For all these many years he had watched over her and her family. She had learned well and had raised 3 great children.

They enjoyed the fresh chocolate chip cookies and milk and laughed about their many adventures. When it was time to go home, the brothers ran down the path, telling the dragon they would see him again soon. Sara and Mother remained with the dragon for a moment. "Thank you, Mr. Dragon, for taking such good care of my children and teaching them the wise ways."

The dragon bowed and said, "It has been an honor to watch over you all."

Sara hugged the dragon and said, "Thank you, Mr. Dragon for all you have taught me. I will never forget you."

The dragon replied, "Dear Sara, you have learned well and you have saved me many times. I am not sure you will remember me, but I know you will always remember these lessons."

"It took my mom some time to remember her adventures with you and my uncle. But she did. I will work each day to remember you. Farewell, and I hope that some day you will be there for my children."

They all hugged each other and then the girl skipped down the yellow path for the last time. She climbed the spiral staircase and she was able to squeeze through the door into her yard. Mother appeared in the tree fort and climbed down to be with her children. They all walked to the house together hand in hand. And Mother said, "Yes, children, there really are such things as dragons!"

Sara's Journal

It was a dark and stormy summer night with a driving rain. Thunder and lightning crashed about the house. The mountain was silhouetted with each flash. The two children were getting ready for bed and they went to the window to watch the storm. Zoe and George were amazed by the bright flashes of lightning.

As the lightning flashed across the mountain, Zoe saw a strange blue light glowing along the mountain trail. "Look! What do you think that is?"

George and Zoe decided they needed to find. out what that glowing blue light was, so they put on their raincoats, grabbed their flashlights, and went out on the muddy trail. As they climbed the mountain, the rain came down and the thunder roared above their heads. The trail was so muddy and they often slipped as they climbed.

They reached a large boulder in the path and the blue glowing light bocamo brighter. It seemed to have a slow, pulsating rhythm to it. George led the way up to the boulder and then stopped. "Should we go ahead?" he asked his sister.

"Of course, what do you think we will find, a dragon or something?"

"Why don't you go first?" he suggested.

"Then let's do this together!"

They held hands and rounded the boulder. They saw a huge dragon lying there in the path. He was glowing a blue color and he looked very sick. The dragon was moaning and his tongue was hanging out of his mouth. The children rushed through the mud to the dragon's side. "Oh, Mr. Dragon, what is the matter with you?"

The rain came down and the thunder and lightning continued. The dragon moaned again. "Dear children, I have eaten some red berries that have made me very sick. I am losing my magical powers. My stomach hurts so bad."

The children were amazed at the size of the dragon. He was the size of three cars! They wanted to help him. George stood up and said, "I know what to do. I'll be right back."

He raced down the muddy trail and back into the house. He ran to the bathroom medicine cabinet and got the bottle of that pink stuff for upset stomachs and ran back to the mountain. The rain was coming down even harder now and the lightning was crashing and the trail was a muddy mess, but George ran ahead determined to help the dragon.

Zoe was sitting next to the moaning dragon telling him everything would be OK as soon as George returned. George came running through the mud and up to the dragon and gave him the bottle. "We never take this medicine without our parents' permission, but you are not a kid! Since you're so big, you should drink the whole bottle. You'll feel better in no time!"

The dragon eyed the pink liquid and then with one big gulp he emptied the bottle. As the children watched over him, he began to return to his natural color, a beautiful green hue. The children were amazed as he changed. Gradually his arms and legs began to move and soon he sat up and spread his wings. "I feel so much better. Thank you, children. Let me stop this crazy storm." The dragon pointed at the sky with his large claw. The children couldn't believe what they saw. The rain stopped, the clouds blew away, and the stars came out.

The dragon turned to the children. "May I ask you who you are and where you are from?"

"My name is Zoe and this is my younger brother, George. We live in the old farmhouse down there below the mountain. We come here all the time. This is one of our most favorite places. But we have never seen you here before. Who are you and where did you come from?"

"I am the dragon and I don't really have a name or a home. I wander the earth looking for friends and a place to call home."

"Well, you've come to the right place, Mr. Dragon! This mountain is a terrific place to live and we'll be your friends. What kind of a house do you live in?"

"Zoe, dragons don't live in houses!" George pointed out. "They live in caves and we have never found any caves here on this mountain."

The dragon thought Zoe's invitation was a marvelous idea. "Children, this is terrific! I have found some great new friends and a wonderful place to live. I will find a cave and then you can visit me."

"But how will we find your cave?" asked Zoe. "And how will we know where to find you?"

"Do you see that big oak tree in your backyard?" The dragon pointed to their backyard and the large oak tree began to glow! The children stared with large eyes. "Whenever you want to come see me, knock three times on that tree and a magic door will open. Climb down the spiral stairs and follow the yellow path to my cave. I will be there waiting for you. Now you need to get home to bed and get some rest. Tomorrow will be another exciting day and I will see you soon. And thank you so much for coming to my rescue."

The children said goodbye to the dragon and climbed down the muddy trail to their house. They hung their wet clothes in the bathroom and climbed into their beds. Zoe asked, "Did we really see a dragon tonight, or have I been dreaming?"

George replied, "Well, if we imagined all of this then we were both dreaming the same dream. There was the rain, the thunder and lightning, and that muddy path! I am pretty sure we found a sick dragon and made him well. We'll try the oak tree in the morning and we'll see if we have found a new friend."

The children fell asleep dreaming of the amazing adventures they would have with their dragon. In the morning, they raced down to a breakfast of pancakes and gooey syrup and big glasses of orange juice. Their mother, Sara, was eyeing them suspiciously. "So I found a lot of wet clothes in the bathroom this morning. What have you two been up to?"

The children explained about the light on the mountain during the storm, climbing up to the boulder, and finding a dragon who they cured with the pink medicine. Sara looked at them and said, "Well children, there just might be some things like dragons!" They both looked at her with wide eyes. They finished up their breakfast and ran to the tree. Sara watched from the kitchen window as her children knocked on the tree three times, the little door opened, and they were on their way.

And then Sara smiled to herself and remembered. She reached into one of the kitchen cabinets and found an old leather diary. She held it close as she remembered her adventures with the dragon and she was glad her old friend had returned to teach her children the dragon's ways. And so the circle was complete and the generations of Sara's family would continue to learn from Mr. Dragon in his cave on the mountain. All was well in her world.

Made in the USA
Lexington, KY
05 November 2019